The
Inch
Prince

Retold by Russell Punter

Illustrated by Matt Ward

Reading Consultant: Alison Kelly
Roehampton University

This is the Inch Prince. If you
measure him, you'll see he's just
one inch tall (that's 2.5cm).

Once upon a time, there was a little old man and a little old woman.

Their names were Mr. and Mrs. Ping.

They lived in a tiny house
by a river.

Every day, they weeded the plants in their vegetable plot...

The beans look beautiful.

fed the animals in their field...

The hens look happy.

and watered the flowers in their garden.

The lilies look lovely.

They had everything they wanted... well, almost.

At that moment, a fairy
flew by.

She heard what Mr. and
Mrs. Ping said.

She noticed their lovely
vegetables...

happy animals...

and tall
flowers.

"These people are kind,"
thought the fairy. "I'll be
kind to them."

She waved her wand and
whispered some magic words.

Jumping beans and flying fish,
Give these folk their
dearest wish.

11

Soon afterwards, Mr.
and Mrs. Ping had a teeny
weeny boy.

In fact, he
was just one
inch tall!

"Let's call him Issun-boshi," said Mrs. Ping.

"Or Issy, for short," said her husband. "Um, very short."

Each year, the Pings' vegetables grew better...

their animals grew bigger...

and their flowers grew taller.

Many years later, it was
time for Issy to leave home.

His parents gave him three
presents for his journey.

18

He had a rice bowl for
a boat.

He had
a pair of
chopsticks
for oars.

And he had a
needle for a sword.

Issy set off down
the river...

between tall

mountains...

past

villages...

around wide woods...

and through
towns...

until he reached
the big city.

"I'll ask the emperor for a job," thought Issy.

"That's if I don't get squashed first."

22

At last, Issy reached
the emperor's
palace.

Two guards were marching
up and down outside.

"I'd like a job," said Issy.

"You're teeny," said one
guard. "What can *you* do?"

"I can run past you for a start," said Issy.

Hey! Where did he go?

He jumped over the guard's foot and ran into the palace.

A cook was making dinner.
"I'd like a job," said Issy.

"You're tiny," said the
cook. "What can *you* do?"

"I can run past you for a start," Issy said.

Hey! Where did he go?

He ran around the cook's oven and into the next room.

Issy was in the throne room. He bowed to the emperor and the princess.

"I'd like a job, please, Your Majesty," said Issy.

"Would you, indeed?"
said the emperor.

"He's teeny-weeny, Daddy,"
said Princess Chi-Chi. "What
can *he* do?"

31

"Well, I ran past your
guard, your maid and your
cook to get here," said Issy.

The emperor thought for a
moment. "You can look after
Princess Chi-Chi," he said.

32

"But Daddy," moaned the princess. "He's only one inch tall."

"Small things can be special too," said the emperor.

From then on, Issy never left the princess's side. He was there in the morning.

He was there in the afternoon.

He was there at night.

One day, the princess
left the palace to visit
her aunt.

Palace ◄

Issy went too.

They came to a dark forest.
"I'm scared," said Princess
Chi-Chi.

"I'll look after you," said Issy.
"What could *you* do?" said
the princess.

Just then, there was a
terrifying roar.

RAAAGGGHH!

HELP!

A giant ogre crashed
through the trees. He reached
out to grab the princess.

“Put her down!” said Issy. “Or I’ll...”

“You?” said the ogre. “What could *you* do?”

The ogre scooped up
Issy, and popped him in
his mouth.

Issy thought quickly.
He took his
needle-sword
and pricked the
ogre's tongue.

OoooWWWW!

Take that!

The ogre spat out Issy and
ran off.

That will
teach him.

Thank you,
Issy.

"Look," said Issy, "the ogre
left his hammer behind."

41

The princess tried to pick it up, but it was too heavy.

Whew, it's heavier than it looks.

"I wish you were bigger, Issy," she said. "Then maybe you could lift it."

42

A cloud of magical stars
shot out of the hammer and
swept around Issy.

Issy felt himself changing.

He grew bigger...

and **bigger**...

and **bigger**.

In seconds, he was as big as the princess.

"I'm as tall as you!" said Issy. "The hammer granted your wish."

The princess fell in love with Issy, but not because he was tall. She loved him because he was brave.

They got married and lived in a house next to the palace.

The house was small,
but Prince Issy and Princess
Chi-Chi were happy.

They both knew that small
things can be special too.

The Inch Prince is based on a
very old Japanese fairy tale
called *The One Inch Boy.*

Series editor: Lesley Sims

First published in 2008 by Usborne Publishing Ltd., Usborne House,
83-85 Saffron Hill, London EC1N 8RT, England. www.usborne.com
Copyright © 2008 Usborne Publishing Ltd.